Beside the River Styx

Helen Vivienne Fletcher

...

ISBN:
978-1-9911980-3-7 (Paperback)
978-1-9911980-4-4 (Epub)
978-1-9911980-5-1 (Large Print)

...

Previous Publication Acknowledgements:

- *There Had Always Been Bones in The Park* first appeared in *Noir Worries* by Milan
- *The Library* was first published in *The Art of Being Human* edited by Tehani Croft and Stephanie Lai, Fablecroft Publishing 2022
- *He Who Laughs Last* was first published in *Dark Deeds Down Under* edited by Craig Sisterson, Clan Destine Press 2022

- *Beside the River Sticks* was first published in *Sproutlings: A Compendium of Little Fictions,* edited by Morgan Bell, Invisible Elephant Press 2017
- *The Night Village* was first broadcast on RadioActive in association with Crip the Lit and VERB Festival 2023

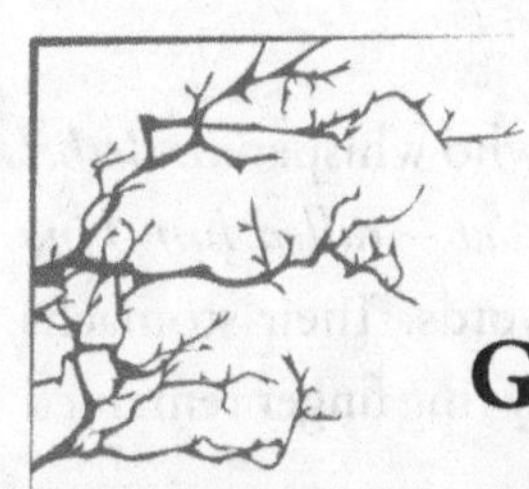

Goblin Mother

We learned the words as children, chanting them as we skipped – *Call on blessed Mary; Spit once for luck; Don't forget to sneeze, ah-tissue, ah-tissue; Bless you to keep the devil out.*

Our mothers tutted and boxed our ears. Evil girls, they'd say. *You'll have cursed babies, the lot of you!*

The other girls gasped and crossed themselves, but I poked out my tongue. *I'll have the evilest baby of them all. He'll be king of the goblins!*

Then it was the mothers' turn to gasp and cross themselves.

You see, I had a secret. I didn't believe in goblins. They were an excuse, a reason to shame women whose babies withered inside them. Someone to blame when a child took only a hundred breaths.

She made a wish... the women would whisper. I learned to whisper too, lest their side-eye be turned on me.

I wish... I wish...

I wished malicious tongues and eyes were the only evils I would face.

As we grew, the other girls stopped skipping. Proper little wives, they folded their hands, dropped their gaze, and said their prayers. No more calling on goblins, they tutted and blessed, and crossed themselves, all without raising their eyes from the ground at their feet.

But me... I never lowered mine.

The other girls, they became the ones who whispered. *Bethel cursed her own unborn baby, don't you know – called him king of the goblins!* I ignored their muttered words. Their stomachs swelled with babes, but mine stayed flat. My ring finger remained unchained.

The girls... the women... they weren't the ones I should have been watching.

The men circled me. Called me ungodly while leering in ungodly ways. They loved me in private and hated themselves for it in the light of day.

When my stomach began to swell, they all denied it.

Unnatural... they all said. *Made a wish and brought a goblin to her bed.*

The whispers turned to mutters. Perhaps goblin was just a name for the things they wanted to forget.

My son was born in the witching hour, and that sealed our fate. They no longer lowered their voices or their eyes. It was no longer luck that made them spit.

Wicked girl, she's brought evil to us all.

They said I cursed my baby, but I loved more than their "godly" hearts ever could. I ran with the babe, taking him far into the forest. They followed, fervour driving them after us. I didn't believe in goblins, but I believed in man even less.

When I could run no further, and the babe weighed heavy in my arms, I spoke the words we had learned as children.

I wish... I wish...

The goblins came from the underground, twisted figures snatching my baby into the night. The men watched him go in silence, no blessing loud enough to keep the devil out.

I'll have the evilest baby of them all, I once told them. *He'll be king of the goblins!*

They pretend they don't remember, but I know they'll never forget.

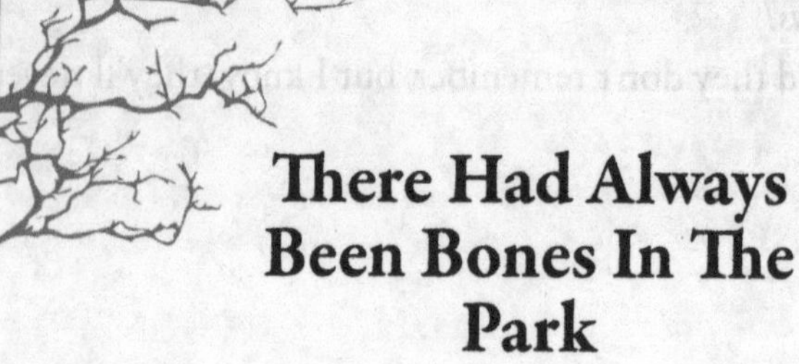

There Had Always Been Bones In The Park

There had always been bones in the park.

Chicken, of course, but it wasn't hard to imagine them as fingers, freed from their flesh encasement long ago and now crunched between her dog's jaws. She didn't know who was consuming these large quantities of drumsticks, or why they felt the need to discard the waste in the grass. But the bones were always there, nonetheless.

Perhaps that's why it wasn't such a surprise when she found the body.

It was an icy morning. That wasn't important, but as her breath turned to smoke around her, a small part of her recognised, and was thankful for, the small mercy of the chill keeping flesh cold.

It took her a while to understand what she was seeing. There was a shoe – presumably a foot inside – and close to that, the cuff of a pair of jeans. Both lay on the green, spongy safety mat, as the gentle to and fro of the swing squeaked above them.

Her dog didn't bark. She had imagined that in situations like these, a dog would bark, frantically pawing and growling at the ground, morphing instantly into a cadaver dog, sensing and locating death.

Instead, he sniffed at the bushes as she stood and stared at the shoe.

Eventually, she forced her eye to travel up and further to the left. There, she saw a face, a pair of open eyes. Then she heard a scream which she thought might have been her own.

When the police officers arrived, she told them about the bones. She made a point of saying they were probably chicken, but she had never seen finger bones, you see? She didn't want to miss something which could have been important.

She kept thinking how the red on his forehead was the same red as her jacket. It felt wrong – too bold and garish, like she had turned up to a funeral in a brightly coloured cocktail dress.

A police officer wrapped a blanket around her and said comforting things. She couldn't quite make out the words, but the tone brushed over her, softly, softly, and she found herself soothed anyway.

Later – she couldn't be sure how much later – she looked down, and there was a paper cup full of tea in her hands. She had a keep cup in her bag. She thought of transferring the liquid into it, but it seemed a little late for saving the environment from this particular paper cup.

Samson licked her face. She tried to find comfort in the gesture, but all she could think of was those bones, crunching between his jaws. She did note that she was now sitting – that she must be for her dog to be able to lick her face – and that he still hadn't barked. Looking at him now, his small, woolly body attempting to climb into her lap, it seemed ridiculous that she had thought him capable of carrying out the tasks of a bloodhound. She picked him up, noting that he was shivering, just as disturbed by the death as she was.

There were more people in the park now. The boy's body was still lying there. She could say that now – his body. He was not just a shoe or an open pair of eyes, he was a person. A dead person, who she had found.

"How are you doing, now?"

The police officer startled her. His voice was suddenly very loud and real, unlike the shushing sounds from the comforting words earlier. His accent was Irish, lilting musically even in just that simple phrase, and she wondered if they had sent him to talk to her for that reason. His words were calming, no matter what he said.

"Yes, I'm okay." Her own voice sounded hoarse, and she suspected she had screamed more than once. "I think I may be in shock."

The police officer smiled slightly, as if glad she had acknowledged it. "Can you tell me your name?"

She blinked, realising he had asked her that before, and she had been unable to answer. "Jennifer. My name is Jennifer."

The police officer gave another slight smile, his relief at her newfound coherence evident. "We will need you to make a full statement, Jennifer. Are you all right to stay a while longer?"

She nodded. "I need to call my boss, though. Tell her why I'm late."

He touched her shoulder gently as he left her to make her call. Jennifer stared at her phone for several minutes, then sent a text instead. She felt incapable of verbalising what had happened.

As a social worker, there had always been a possibility she would one day find someone's body – a client overdose or suicide; a domestic situation spun out of control. She'd thought about it every time she knocked on a door and it took more than a few seconds for someone to answer. But that still hadn't prepared her for finding a teenager dead in a playground.

She made her statement, repeating everything she had told them earlier, but more intelligibly. She left out the bones this time, feeling silly for having mentioned them in the first place.

There were more people in the park now, gathered around the edges of the cordon. She picked up Samson, afraid someone would step on him, and the police officer lifted the tape for her to duck under. The crowd parted as if wary of touching her. For once, she was not the calm presence helping to defuse the bad situation. Instead, she was a part of it. His death would always be a piece of her story.

A girl stepped forward, blocking Jennifer's way. She had been crying, but her face also displayed something else.

"Please," the girl said. "Do you know what happened?"

No one had expressly told Jennifer she shouldn't tell anyone, but more than that, she realised she didn't really know. She shook her head, and the girl closed her eyes, pressing shaking hands to her lips.

Jennifer recognised the self-shushing gesture, and the nature of the girl's pain. In her work, she had come to know there were two types of guilt. There was the useful type – the one that got you answers, where someone knew or had done something. And then there was the illogical kind, the self-blame.

"He messaged me to come meet him," the girl whispered. "I didn't see it until this morning."

Jennifer knew she should direct the girl to speak to the police, or at least say something comforting. "Maybe he fell," she said instead. It was not the soothing statement she had hoped to come out with.

In her mind, she saw him trip on the edge of the safety mat, his head hitting the metal of the swing-set frame. It would be the most innocuous of the ways she would imagine his death. Imagining it was not going to be optional.

She touched the girl's shoulder and left the park.

She walked home, like she normally did. Once inside, she peeled the red coat off, and tossed it into the back of the wardrobe, closing the door on it. She made a cup of tea, and for a moment almost forgot the events of the morning.

Samson had brought something back with him, clenched tightly between his teeth. He dropped it on the kitchen floor. She wasn't sure whether he meant it as an offering for her, or if he'd simply lost track of it.

It was a stick, not a bone, but everything would be bones to her now. She stared at it for a long while, studying the splintered wood, noting the indents from Samson's teeth.

Perhaps the police would call her when they found out what had happened; perhaps she would see it on the news. Or perhaps she would never know. He would become another statistic, like the ones she saw on paper every day.

She took a piece of kitchen towel, picked up the saliva-soaked stick and placed it in the bin. She closed the lid and started to cry.

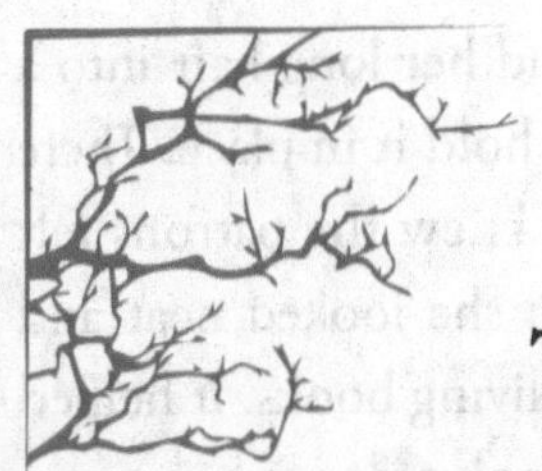

The Library

Kyra woke with black lines drawn on her arms. She stared at them, trying to decipher meaning from the slashes and swirls hurriedly scribbled across her skin. Paper was precious, the dry, acidic air causing it to crack and crumble just like everything else around her, so Kyra often wrote notes to herself on her hands. Words sometimes crept up her wrist or beyond, like insects slithering across her limbs.

She'd been writing before she fell asleep the night before, and it seemed her dreaming-self had continued with a heavy hand, pressing the pen deep into her flesh. The black ink was surrounded by the red of perturbed skin, her letters becoming less and less legible the higher up her arm she got.

Kyra grimaced. Pens were nearly as rare as paper these days, and it was unconscionable to have wasted the ink. She stroked a finger softly along the lines, whispering the words to herself. She imagined this was how people had once felt reading books, coaxing sentences from dark text scratched across pages. But there was no meaning here, only ideas her tired brain had thought were important in the early hours of the morning. She put on a long-sleeved shirt, hiding the writing away.

Sand and ash had gathered in her hair as she slept, blowing in through the gaping hole in her bedroom wall. The dusty colour of her curls hid the particles, but she felt the grit chafing at her skin. She shook the sand free, then wound her long hair into a tight bun, stabbing the pen through it to hold it in place. There was no dress code at the library, but she knew the patrons felt more comfortable approaching her when she looked neat and tidy. Besides, she was the youngest of the living books. It helped to reassure customers if she made herself look older.

She finished getting ready, then wrapped a scarf around her face for protection. Part of the wall crumbled away as she stepped through the gap where her front door used to be. The destruction didn't bother her like it used to; decay was a part of life now.

She lowered her head against the dust storm, pulling her scarf a little higher, then made her way down the street. It was a short walk – one she could do with her eyes closed, which was becoming more and more of a necessity. A scarf could only do so much to protect her skin and eyes from the sandpaper effect of the wind.

THE LIBRARY WAS QUIET. There were no patrons, but more worryingly, most of the living-book chairs were empty too. Kyra felt she could see the knowledge slipping away, like the sand that blew through everything. Hardly anyone checked out the history or science living books now; no one wanted to hear about a past none of them found any meaning in. Besides, no one knew if the narratives they told were true anymore. The histories seemed to have changed from the ones she'd heard as a child, and the books hadn't chosen their successors. Persuading someone to take on all that terrible knowledge seemed more of a tragedy than letting it be forgotten.

Kyra spent the first part of the morning cleaning, trying fruitlessly to keep the dry dust, ash, sand, and all the other particulates she didn't quite have names for, back from the books. The paper books, that was. There was only one other living book there – a tall, thin boy, who sat slumped in his chair, neither ignoring nor helping with her efforts. He wore a pair of glasses with only one lens left, and every so often it would catch the light, almost as if he were winking at her. He didn't seem the type to wink, though – far too serious and lethargic.

The chairs for the living books were set out in a semi-circle up the front, almost like a protective barrier between the library entrance and the paper books. What was left of them. The shelves still held tomes, keeping up the tradition of what libraries had once been, but there were so many gaps now. Most of the paper books had already begun the process of disintegrating, pages drying out and crumbling to nothing. Kyra didn't dare open them, instead gently brushing the dust back, praying she wouldn't further harm their covers with the movement. She wished she could say the living books were faring better; her skin cracked and flaked almost at the same rate as the paper.

"I WANT TO LEARN HOW to sew on a button."

Kyra looked up from her seat in one of the living book chairs. An older woman held a shirt out to the other living book, the boy. Her hands were shaking, a fluttering, repetitive tremor making its way through her core every few seconds. She clutched a red library token in her other palm.

The living book's name was Eric, and he wasn't much older than Kyra, but he seemed to carry a tiredness beyond his age.

He blinked now, as if dumbfounded by the woman's statement. He raised his head, his eyes seeking out Kyra's.

She stood and stepped forward, coming to his rescue. "I can help you with that." She tried to meet the customer's eye, but the woman looked away. The shirt showed signs of having been mended earlier – all the woman's clothes did. Kyra suspected she felt less embarrassed claiming not to know how to sew, than to admitting she no longer could.

"How about you have a seat?" Kyra gave the woman a warm smile. "You can watch me sew these ones."

Eric made the woman a cup of tea, while Kyra stitched. The shirt needed several repairs, so she kept up the pretence of teaching while mending them all. Eric had chosen a mug with a large handle, and placed it carefully in the woman's hands, holding on for an extra moment or two to make sure she had a good grip.

He gave Kyra an embarrassed smile when he saw her watching.

Kyra was not the living book on sewing, but the boy who was had not come to the library in weeks. Kyra had picked up his role, preferring to keep busy than to wait for someone to be interested in hers. It helped to still her mind when her hands had a reason to move.

She finished the shirt, handing it back. The woman's shaking fingers clasped it, but her eyes stayed downcast. She mumbled something which may have been thanks, but all Kyra heard was the rasp of dry air over a reluctant tongue. The woman shuffled away, and Kyra wondered if she might disintegrate into the air in front of them. There seemed such an impermanence to everything now, even the people.

"You should have charged her a blue token," Eric said once she was gone. "You did the work for her."

Kyra shrugged, tossing the red token into the box behind the counter. "Are you going to tell on me?"

Eric stared at her for a moment, and then slowly smiled. "No."

IN THE AFTERNOON, THERE was a younger woman with a ball of wool who wanted a scarf made. She tossed the blue token and the wool at Kyra without even considering learning herself. Kyra thought of telling her she would have to come back when the wool-craft book was available but bit her tongue. She found a pair of needles behind the counter instead. Eric rolled his eyes at Kyra once the lady's back was turned.

He had a little girl come in with a broken radio. She held up her red token eagerly, and Eric sat on the floor with her, showing her how to dismantle it and put the components back together. Kyra was surprised. She'd not thought Eric the type to be so patient or engaged with young children. There was a light in his eyes now, though; a passion as he explained the way things worked.

Kyra set down her knitting at one point to get a glass of water for the girl. A dry cough wracked its way through her small frame. The water wouldn't help much, but Kyra was struck by the need to do something – anything – to make the child more comfortable. Eric frowned every time the girl's little chest shook, the air barking from her in a way that had to be painful. None of them mentioned it, of course. The cough was a pain they had all experienced, but none could fix.

BETWEEN PATRONS, ERIC worked on a project of his own making while Kyra stitched. He was fixing metal pieces together from the box of scrap collected behind the counter. Kyra didn't know if he was allowed to do that, but the silence between them was companionable now, and she didn't want to risk that by asking.

A boy of about ten or twelve came in, a toddler balanced on his hip. His face fell when he saw Kyra and Eric.

"I wanted the baker," he said.

Kyra and Eric looked at each other. The living book on cooking wasn't much in demand. Most people learnt to prepare food in their early years while they still had a parent around. The cooking manual's few patrons were from well-off families, wanting to learn how to make something special.

"She'll be in next week," Eric told the boy, though Kyra wasn't sure that was true.

The child began to scream, and the boy shushed her. From his manner, it seemed like he would have preferred to join her in screaming.

"What were you wanting to learn?" Kyra asked him.

"Bread," said the boy. "And anything cheap."

Eric glanced at Kyra, then down at the knitting in her hands. "I'll teach you," he said.

Kyra joined them in the kitchen, setting the knitting down for a moment to help brush sand from the benches. She rolled up her sleeves to wash her hands, and when she turned back, Eric was staring at her arms. Her cheeks flushed; she had forgotten the scrawled writing on her skin. A frown crossed Eric's face. Then the toddler started to cry again, and they both turned back to her brother. Kyra rolled her sleeves down quickly, hiding her sleep-written nonsense.

Eric set to baking, explaining the steps as he did, and Kyra returned to her knitting. She was near to finishing the scarf now, and she found the rhythm of the stitches calming.

"Are you alone?" she asked the boy.

He nodded. "They're gone."

Neither Kyra nor Eric expressed sympathy, knowing their skills as books would be much more useful to him than any pointless platitudes they could produce. Twelve was old enough to take care of himself – Kyra had been alone since she was eleven, and most were by the time they reached fifteen.

The younger child was another matter. There was a reason most chose not to have a second child. She just hoped the boy survived long enough to give his sibling a chance.

"What's your name?" Eric asked.

The boy blinked, as if he had to think about the answer. Kyra suspected it had been a long time since anyone cared enough to ask his name, let alone use it.

"Thomas," he said finally.

"We can help you with other things, Thomas," she told him, and Eric's head jerked in what she chose to interpret as a nod of agreement. "Just come in when you need."

He had not produced a token; Kyra felt a silent pact forming between her and Eric to never ask.

KYRA WASHED CAREFULLY that night, wanting to preserve the writing on her skin, while still cleansing herself of the atmosphere's grime and dust. She skipped moisturising, knowing it would break down the ink faster. She would probably regret it tomorrow when her body flaked with dry scales of dead skin cells, but in that moment, it felt worth it. Already she was losing the beginnings and endings of words, the story filled with gaps after living for only a few hours.

The night was too warm for sleep, as many were these days. Kyra sat on the couch instead, staring out at the world through the hole in the wall. Her heart raced every time she saw movement, and she spoke calming words to herself, soothing her mind with an invented tale. She didn't write it down this time. The pen twirled between her fingers, but she couldn't justify the ink.

Finally she dozed, not falling into a deep sleep, only closing her eyes long enough to stave off exhaustion.

She woke suddenly to a cracking noise. Her sleep-clouded eyes opened just in time to see a chunk of the roof falling towards her. She dove sideways, grazing her arm on the sand-riddled floor as a chunk of ceiling landed on the cushion where she'd been lying. The couch responded with a twang, breaking yet another spring.

Kyra lay her head back, letting her heart settle. She stared at the new hole in the roof, wondering if the whole ceiling was about to come down on her. There were too many holes already. At least she could see the stars through this one.

"WHAT ARE YOU?" ERIC asked her the next day.

Kyra looked up at the question, frowning as she met Eric's eye.

"Which book, I mean. I know you're not supposed to be doing that." He gestured to the knitting needles beside her.

"No, I'm not the sewing manual." She sighed, wondering if Eric would lose respect for her once he knew. "I'm a story," she told him.

He blinked, surprise rippling over his face. "A story..." He breathed the word, his tone almost reverential.

People didn't often come in for fiction anymore, her words almost as forgotten as the history and science books. The practical skills were far more sought after, and she'd adopted so many of those that people often forgot why she was really there. Perhaps the living books should have had covers, like the paper books used to. Kyra had never seen one in its original state – most of the titles had worn away and the pictures faded, but she could see from the remnants of colours that they had been beautiful once.

"I thought you might have been computers," Eric said.

It was Kyra's turn to blink. "Computers?"

It had been a long time since they'd had a living book on that type of technology. For a while, people had tried to preserve computers like they did the paper books, but in the end the air, and dust and ash had broken all of them down, leaving nothing but parts to be cannibalised into other machinery.

Eric hesitated, then touched her arm, indicating the marks. "It's a code, isn't it?"

Kyra shook her head. She'd only seen a computer a handful of times, and never close enough to try make it work. "It's just messy writing." She pulled up her sleeve, revealing the scrawls. He had seen them already, but she still felt self-conscious showing them. "I was doing it before bed... I guess I sleepwalk."

He stared at her skin for a moment, then reached out, gently running a finger along the lines. Kyra resisted the urge to shiver under his touch. She was not used to physical contact.

"You tell stories even in your sleep," he said softly.

Kyra's cheeks flushed again. She wasn't sure whether he was laughing at her. His hand still rested against her arm, and she pulled away, suddenly afraid to let him read her words.

"No one wants to hear stories anymore," she told him.

KYRA FINISHED MAKING the scarf in the afternoon, though the woman didn't return to pick it up. There was no other work for Kyra to do, so she took to mending her own clothes, applying yet another patch to a shirt that had worn through. Eric put aside the machinery he had been working on, leaning back to stretch.

He watched Kyra for a moment, seeming fascinated by her careful stitches, though she was sure he must know how to sew himself. They'd never talked about their situations, but she guessed he was on his own. It was probably the reason he came to all his shifts, unlike the other living books.

Eric walked over and placed a blue token on the counter beside Kyra.

She frowned at him, wondering if he was making fun of her. He met her gaze levelly, no hint of derision in his eyes.

"I want to hear a story," he told her.

Kyra stared at the token.

Eric sat back down, watching her expectantly. She hesitated. She could say no. The living books always had the right to refuse a customer, though they rarely did when there were so few. Eric waited, calmly, his eyes fixed on hers.

Finally, she put her sewing aside, folding her hands neatly in her lap as she had been taught, a thick feeling growing in her throat despite the dry air. "Which story would you like to hear?" she asked.

"You know more than one?"

Kyra nodded. Her mother had been the storyteller before her, responsible for memorising five books of those chosen to be saved, but she had learned many more, teaching them to Kyra from when she was little. Kyra had always known she would take over the role of storyteller.

It had been a long time since Kyra had spoken a book aloud though.

Eric smiled. "Tell me your favourite."

Kyra cleared her throat, trying to ignore how much the sound resembled the rattle she'd heard in the little girl's chest yesterday.

"Here starts the story about a whale," Kyra said, giving the formal introduction her mother had told her to use, and then she began.

She wasn't sure if the story was really her favourite, but it was the longest story she knew. She could remember most of it... most but not all. It didn't matter. She was sure Eric would grow tired before the end.

The process of telling a story felt strange and awkward to her now; it was so long since she'd done it. But Eric had given his token. He listened quietly, and Kyra found herself analysing even the tiniest changes in his expression, wondering what he was thinking.

"Thank you," he said, as her voice finally petered out at the end of the day.

Kyra nodded, unsure what else to say. She still couldn't tell what he thought. He nodded back, then turned away, leaving her to lock up the library for the night.

Despite the awkwardness, Kyra found herself smiling as she walked home that night, smiling still as she swept sand and ash from her couch and stared up through that hole in the ceiling to the sky. The stars seemed to make the shape of a whale.

ERIC PLACED ANOTHER token on the counter in the morning. Red this time, though Kyra wasn't worried by the colour. The boxes behind the counter were overflowing with both red and blue. The council seemed to have forgotten about the library, leaving it to Kyra's and Eric's care.

"The same story?" Kyra asked. She couldn't shake the feeling he was playing a game with her.

He gave a half smile. "I want to know what happens."

Kyra didn't sit this time, nor fold her hands neatly. The formality of it felt silly when it was just the two of them. Instead, she carried on with the normal morning clean up, brushing away the sand that had slipped under the door overnight, speaking the story as she did. Eric helped her this time, even going so far as to take the broom from her to sweep the floor, while Kyra did her best to protect the books. There was a strange comfort in the routine, though she knew their efforts were a leaking dam, and they were barely holding back the inevitable.

The newsboy arrived during Kyra's telling. He hovered, listening as she wrapped up that part of the story. She knew she was paraphrasing, the original words lost just like the title, and she thought she may have renamed the characters too, though she couldn't be sure.

"I's Artur and I comed to give the weekly newsreporting," the boy told them when Kyra finished.

He rambled through the reports, his use of language hard to understand at times, like it was with many of the newsreporters. They were often orphans, left alone at a young age. The children were chosen for their fitness to travel long distances without tiring, but their level of comprehension of their own reports was often low. Their work also took them through countless towns, across many dialects and accents, and the result was a mish-mash of language.

Somehow, Kyra found it comforting. News of famine and destruction was less frightening when it came with a curious manipulation of words and grammar.

Artur hesitated when he finished, and Kyra wondered if he was hoping for payment.

"Cans I hear your reporting?" he asked Kyra.

"My reporting?"

"He means your story," Eric said quietly.

Kyra flushed, embarrassed that the boy had been listening for long enough to want to hear more. He dug through his pocket, producing a very grubby red token.

Kyra waved it away. "It's okay. Eric has already paid."

Eric seemed amused by this exchange. "I'll make us some tea," he said.

Kyra was glad for the suggestion of liquid. She was no longer used to saying so many words at once.

Artur settled cross-legged on the floor, staring up at her eagerly. He had a smudge of something dark under his right eye, and his thin shoulders poked through the ragged neck of his shirt. She'd heard that before the world had begun to crumble, children used to gather together every day to learn. She couldn't imagine being able to keep so many children in one place for long.

Eric returned from the kitchen with the tea and a plate of bread, which he held out to Artur. Kyra felt something unknot in her stomach as she watched him eat. The child's thin arms made her nervous, though she hadn't quite thought what to do about it. They weren't supposed to feed patrons unless they produced a token for the cooking living book, and she didn't feel right taking the child's last one.

Eric met her eye, and acknowledgement of this latest small act of rebellion passed between them.

Artur fell on the bread, hungrily stuffing it into his mouth as he peered up at Kyra, still waiting for her to begin.

"Leave some tea for Kyra," Eric told him. "She'll need it to tell the story."

THE NEWSBOY STAYED while Kyra spoke the next chapter. She called them chapters, but she had never seen the pages, so she just paused at the logical stopping points.

There were many words Kyra didn't know the meaning of. She could have skipped them, paraphrasing as she knew she was doing with other parts of the story. Strangely, these unfamiliar terms were the parts she remembered the most. In her mind, she could see her mother's lips moving as they slid over the words, getting Kyra to repeat them back to her.

Kyra's voice caught a little as she thought about her mother. Each sentence seemed to echo in the air around her, as if Kyra were still a child, sitting in her mother's lap, the narrative dancing in the air above her head. Teaching Kyra the book hadn't just kept the story alive – in this moment, it was like her mother was there reading too.

Eric sensed her faltering, as her words disappeared with the emotion of remembering. His eyes found hers, and he nodded once, the light glinting off the one lens of his broken glasses. Kyra nodded back, and found her way to finishing the chapter with that small encouragement.

The newsboy gave her a big smile, exposing a greying dead tooth. "That was some good reporting. Thanking you. I'll comes for more listening formorrow."

Kyra flushed, pleased this time rather than embarrassed. She watched from the doorway as he raced off down the street, back to his news route. She wondered if he would adopt some of the story of the whale, adding it into his daily reports in his confused and chaotic way. The idea pleased her more than it should have.

WHEN THE FIRST PATRON of the day arrived, Kyra automatically stopped her telling, but Eric urged her to keep going. The customer seemed confused by it, but he stayed long after Eric had finished working on his clock, listening. Kyra was not yet used to storytelling to even one person, let alone a group, but the man's stillness and focused attention made her want to continue.

He must have been in his forties, old by the current life expectancy, but his tired, dark-circle-rimmed eyes watched Kyra with an intensity similar to Artur's. Kyra found she couldn't look at him directly without growing self-conscious and losing her place, so she focused on Eric instead. He was the one paying the token, after all.

"My father used to tell me stories," the man said, when Kyra paused for breath.

Kyra noticed his hands were shaking, as he clutched the clock Eric had fixed for him. She wasn't sure whether it was from illness or emotion, but she felt compelled to reach out, gently touching his hand.

The man moved as if to withdraw from her, then he let out a breath and smiled at Kyra. The whites of his eyes were tie-dyed with red streaks. Kyra hadn't heard him cough, but eyes like that were usually a sign of a lifetime of fighting against broken lungs.

"I'm going to keep reading," Kyra told him. "You can come back again if you like."

The man's face lit up at the idea. "Thank you. I think I will."

Kyra suspected she wouldn't see the man again. She liked that the thought of it had made him happy, though. Maybe just the idea of having somewhere to go and listen to a story was enough.

ERIC TENDED TO ALL of the library patrons that day, as Kyra continued speaking. He hesitated when a woman came in with more sewing, but Kyra reached for it, barely pausing for breath. She had always been good at multitasking, and she felt less self-conscious when she had something to do with her hands.

Each customer lingered to listen to Kyra's words. It wasn't quite a crowd, no one staying for long enough for a group to form, but somehow each tarrying person made the library feel fuller, and more alive.

THE LADY WITH THE SCARF came back. Kyra was nearing the end of a chapter, so she kept speaking, knowing she would be finished soon.

The woman glanced around at the people listening and frowned. She stood for a moment, the crease in her forehead deepening, then she cleared her throat loudly, cutting Kyra off mid-sentence.

"Excuse me," she said. "I'm here to pick up my scarf."

The other library patrons looked around, blinking as they came out of the world of the story.

"Yes, of course." Kyra moved to collect the scarf from behind the counter, but Eric was already there, handing it to her.

"What's all this then?" the woman asked as Kyra gave her the scarf.

"A story," Kyra told her.

The woman glanced around again and sniffed. She held herself tightly, her mouth and shoulders pinched, as if everything in life made her angry. "Not really worth keeping people waiting for that, is it?"

Kyra's face flushed. She wanted to turn away, but the woman raised her eyebrows, waiting for an answer. After a morning of speaking, Kyra suddenly found she had no words. Out of the corner of her eye, she saw Eric stepping forward, ready to come to her defence, but it was one of the library patrons who spoke.

"Leave the girl alone. We're enjoying it." The man gave Kyra a wink. His skin was raised into a red rash, his face reacting to the sandpaper effect of the wind outside, but he smiled at Kyra despite the cracks that appeared at the corners of his mouth with the movement.

Another patron nodded for her to continue. "Come on, love," she said. "Tell us the next part."

Kyra looked between the scarf-lady and the other library customers, her stomach swirling with anxiety under the woman's disapproving gaze. The interruption had caused her to lose her place and forget the lines of the story.

Then she caught sight of Eric. He mouthed the last words she had spoken. She let out a breath, surprised he had been listening so closely as to remember, but she was grateful, nonetheless.

Kyra nodded her thanks, then repeated the line aloud, carrying on with the story. The scarf-lady made a disapproving noise in her throat, but she didn't interrupt again, and when Kyra next looked up, she was gone.

ERIC WALKED PART OF the way home with Kyra that night. She was tired, her throat dry and scratchy, and the mental energy of remembering the story had drained her. He seemed to understand, filling the silence himself, saying more than Kyra had ever heard from him before. His words flowed over her, the meaning not quite reaching her through her exhaustion.

Finally, they came to a crossroads, and Eric raised his hand in farewell. "See you tomorrow, Kyra," he said, before turning in the other direction.

Kyra didn't give him a goodbye, a fact she only became conscious of after she had taken a few steps down the path. She glanced back, regretting her rudeness, but he was already gone.

Kyra hesitated outside her house. Pieces of broken rubble were scattered outside the hole that served as a doorway – more than had been there when she left that morning.

She peered inside, knowing it probably meant looters had been through again. Fear bubbled up in her stomach, and she glanced back, half hoping Eric would reappear. The street behind her remained empty.

She took a breath. The looting didn't matter really, she told herself. There hadn't been a lot inside to steal, or at least, not a lot that would stay whole. All her possessions were so broken down by the atmosphere, sometimes falling apart if she so much as touched them. But it was still unsettling to know someone had been inside her home.

She took another, deeper, breath, steeling herself for whatever might be waiting for her, then stepped through the gap in the wall.

Kyra had kept a few things after her parents died, more out of the habit her mother had started than any real emotional connection to them. Most objects had begun breaking down long before Kyra's memories of them had formed, and she held no real attachment to them.

She couldn't say the same of the items the looters had taken. They'd left her with no moisturiser, no food; all the practical amenities stripped away. The larger pieces of furniture remained, though some had been tossed, presumably as the looters searched crevices for hidden items of value.

The only one of those was the pen stabbed into Kyra's hair. She touched it now, reassuring herself.

They had not broken the door to her parents' room, though. The only room in the house with four solid walls still standing, a sturdy lock on the door, the key always in her pocket.

Kyra should have moved on when the walls began to crack, but perhaps there was a level of sentimentality in her after all. Leaving would have felt like a goodbye she wasn't ready to make. Besides, where would she go? This house was hers, even if it were in pieces. She lay down on the floor and stared at the stars.

THOMAS WAS WAITING outside the library when Kyra arrived the next morning, his sister balanced on his hip again. His cheeks looked thinner. Eric stood with him, and his eyes sought out Kyra's.

He leaned over to whisper to her. "I think he just wants somewhere to go."

Kyra nodded. Twelve was young to be alone with a child.

They ushered him inside, Eric beginning the process of making tea almost like it was a ritual or act of worship rather than just the preparation of a drink. He brought out the mugs, handing one to each of them. Kyra sipped hers, more for something to do than from any desire to drink, though of course she was thirsty. She was always parched in the dry air; there wasn't enough liquid left in the world to solve that problem.

"Do you know they used to drink this hot?" Eric asked Thomas.

Kyra glanced down at the mug of cool liquid in her hands, wondering how anyone could bear swallowing hot water. She had heard that the temperature outside used to be cooler, though she couldn't imagine that either.

"How odd," she mumbled, because Thomas had not yet answered.

Eric looked from her to Thomas, then reached into his pocket. He placed a blue token on the counter, raising his eyebrows at Kyra.

"What about...?" She tilted her head towards the boy, and the child playing at his feet.

"I think they could use the distraction," Eric said. "Besides," he nodded towards the door, "I'm not the only one who wants to hear it."

Kyra turned, finding Artur hovering half inside. He grinned, a gap-tooth smile lighting his face when he saw her. The dead tooth must have come loose.

"I comes to hear your reporting," Artur told her. "And I bringed mine friend, Jenni."

Behind him stood the little girl whose radio Eric had helped mend. She looked thinner too, but she gave Kyra a shy smile.

Kyra swallowed. They were all so small – little lost children, barely surviving in this world. A story about a whale wasn't going to solve that, and Eric was kidding himself if he thought otherwise.

KYRA SPOKE THE STORY with more confidence now, letting her body move where it felt appropriate to stand or pace, embellishing the drama when she knew she had their attention.

Artur and Jenni joined in with sound effects, shrieking with excitement during the action and shushing like the waves of an ocean none of them had ever seen.

Eric picked up the toddler, giving her brother a break. At first, Thomas didn't seem to notice. When he did finally register she was gone, he raised his head, panic flitting across his face until he saw the child safe in Eric's arms.

Thomas seemed to wake up after that. He watched Kyra speak, his eyes tracking her as she moved, though sometimes they would glaze over again, as he slipped back inside his own thoughts.

Every so often, Kyra would be interrupted by Jenni's cough. It seemed to ease a little with the copious cups of tea Eric handed her, but it was still there, punctuating Kyra's words.

Cups of tea and stories. It still seemed a feeble offering in the face of the disintegrating world. At least the library had four solid walls. Perhaps that was enough to give these children.

Artur and Jenni left after an hour or so, growing tired of sitting still. They both promised to return "formorrow", and Kyra smiled at the word. She saw Eric doing the same.

Throughout the day, Kyra always had an audience, though she didn't think the story would make much sense, hearing only pieces. No one seemed to mind. It had been so long since many of them had heard fiction. The only ones who stayed the whole time were Eric, Thomas, and his little sister.

Finally, her throat grew dry, and she knew it was time to head home. She finished the chapter then paused, letting the library fall into silence.

Thomas stayed in his zoned-out state for a moment, then he blinked, recognising that Kyra had stopped talking. He cleared his throat. "Thank you," he said simply. He reached out, taking his sister from Eric.

He made his way over to the door, then turned back. "Can I... can I come again?"

Kyra nodded. "Of course."

"Every day, if you want," Eric added.

KYRA WOKE IN THE MIDDLE of the night. She could hear voices outside; drunken laughter carried through the hole in her wall, and a hand appeared, creeping around the side of the doorway.

Kyra sucked in a breath. She wanted to scream – of course she wanted to scream – but instead she moved quickly, silently, stealing away to her parents' room and locking the door behind her.

For a moment, she imagined her mother there on the other side of the door, wrapping warm arms around her, her father's strong voice yelling for the strangers to leave. Instead, the only comfort was the room itself.

Kyra closed herself inside, climbing under the bed covers. She wanted to pretend her mother's scent still lingered in the blankets but breathing in only filled her mouth and nose with dust and ash and sand, the same as every breath she had ever taken.

Muffled scraping sounds filled the room as the men made their way into the house, then a crash and more drunken laughter. Kyra willed herself to stay still and silent, but her lungs heaved. A hacking cough barked out from her.

The laughter outside the door stopped, and she heard the men coming closer. She buried her face in the blankets, trying to deaden the sound, but the coughs kept coming.

"Is there a little mousey in this housey?" one of the men called out.

The walls shook as they tried the door, dust and flakes of paint cascading down. "Come out, little mousey, come on out."

Kyra didn't move. A few more hours and it would be light. Like rats, the men would slink away when the daylight exposed them, only willing to gnash their teeth under the cover of darkness.

Thuds crashed against the walls, sending more dust trails skittering down to Kyra. At one point, she reached up for her pen, not to write but for the comfort of holding it. But she realised her hair was loose, the bun and its adornment gone. Her eyes burned with the realisation of the loss, and she curled tighter under the blanket.

The door is strong, Kyra told herself. A few hours, until dawn – she could survive curled up in here that long.

I'm safe. The door is strong. She only wished she could say the same of the walls.

EVENTUALLY THE NOISES stopped, but Kyra slept only fitfully, her ears and body on high alert. She'd heard thieves often waited, coming back when homeowners had started to return to normality, replacing the food and other items that had been stolen, just in time to be stolen again. She guessed that's what they'd been trying to do this time, but she had been at the library, no time to replace anything.

Kyra's stomach growled at the thought of food. It was morning now, and her throat begged for water. She moved to the door, but couldn't bring herself to open it. She stood, instead, with her palm pressed against the wood, listening... listening... listening. There was nothing, but how could she trust the silence?

Screwing up her courage, Kyra took a deep breath, and then another, before turning the key in the lock. But no amount of breathing could prepare her for the sight when she opened the door. The couch had been stripped of fabric, its broken frame left halfway out the doorway. Everything else was gone. A new hole had appeared in the wall, and what was left seemed to shiver with the anticipation of falling.

This was not a home anymore, nor even a house. The sand and dust and ash had piled up, burying the remains of her possessions. She trod carefully, wanting to breathe in as little as possible.

Something cracked beneath her feet. Kyra froze, her nerves tense, preparing for attack, but none came. She knelt down, pushing the sand back to uncover what she'd broken, then cradled the pieces of her pen carefully, trying to fit them back together as the ink spilled out over her hands, staining them black.

KYRA STAYED IN THE house, locking herself in her parents' room again at night, though she wasn't really fooling herself that it gave her any more security than being out in the open.

The next morning she tried to make a plan, but instead just found herself sitting on the ground, staring at the destruction. She watched as pieces crumbled from the walls and flakes shed from her dry skin. Perhaps soon she would turn to dust, and she wouldn't have to worry anymore about what to do.

"Kyra."

She looked up, too tired to be startled by the figure in the doorway hole. The light had changed, the murky shadows of afternoon settling in, making her question how long she had been sitting there.

Eric moved forward, sinking to his knees beside her. "Are you all right?"

Kyra just shook her head. She wasn't all right and hadn't been for a long time. Eric's eyes scanned the room, taking in the destruction. He didn't ask what had happened, there was no need. It was the same thing that had happened everywhere.

"Why are you here?" she asked him.

He drew his focus back to her, blinking. "You didn't come to the library."

"I wasn't rostered on." This was true, but only because Kyra was the one supposed to draw up the rosters. She hadn't bothered these last few weeks, as more and more living books had stopped coming. Only she and Eric turned up regularly, and they didn't need a roster to tell them when that should be.

Eric fell quiet. Why was it that the two of them had kept showing up, even when they didn't have to? They were the youngest of the living books, and yet somehow the responsibility of keeping the library running had fallen to them.

"They still came," Eric said eventually.

"Who?"

"The people who've been listening." Eric held her eye. "They came, even though you didn't."

Kyra thought of Thomas trying to care for his sister; Artur, the newsboy, and little Jenni with the wracking cough. There were others too who had come each day, adults and children alike, all wanting to hear something outside of their own lives.

Kyra hadn't learnt the other names, finding it hard enough to keep all the details of the story in her mind without adding remembering a crowd. It felt callous now, to have not even tried. She should have learned some of their stories, instead of just reciting the one she had memorised.

"You should come back," Eric said. "They miss you. I miss you."

"I'm scared," she said.

She hadn't meant to tell him that, but it was true. She was scared to leave, the short walk from her house to the library feeling impossible with the voices of the looters echoing inside her mind. If she was honest, she was scared to stay here too. Whether it was from the looters returning, or the ceiling collapsing down on her, she would die in this house if she didn't get out soon.

Eric hesitated, then he reached out, gently slipping his hand into hers. The feeling of physical contact was still strange to Kyra, but she was glad of it. She squeezed his hand and felt comfort in his responding grip.

"I'll stay here tonight," he told her. "Then we'll go back to the library tomorrow."

Kyra stared at their hands, the black ink from hers transferring to him, marking his palm. "Okay," she said, with more confidence than she felt.

It probably wasn't safe for them to stay here, even just for the night, and he didn't comment on what they would do after that. But for now, it was enough of a plan.

"I DON'T KNOW THE ENDING."

Eric had walked her home after the library patrons had left for the day. She'd been tired, not wanting to talk after speaking all day, but he'd made no move to leave, simply settling into the chaos of her wrecked house. Now he waited, giving her space to elaborate.

"The whale story," she said. "It's been a long time since I told it, and I don't remember the ending."

The patrons had been excited to see her that morning, waiting for her just as Eric had described. Artur and Jenni had raced up to hug her, and Kyra wondered if either of them had anyone to look after them. It seemed like all the people who came were alone.

She pictured all those lost souls now, and how disappointed they would be when her words came to an abrupt stop. Not just disappointed; she feared they would be angry with her for wasting their time.

Eric frowned. "It's in the library somewhere, isn't it? The book?"

"Yes, but..." Kyra shook her head. The book would start to disintegrate the moment she opened it. "It will fall apart, then it will be gone forever."

Eric was quiet for a long time. He traced a pattern into the sand on the floor, though the wind shifted it under his hands, his drawing even less permanent than the ink on Kyra's palms.

"Books were made to be read," he said finally.

He was right, though it was hard for her to admit. What was the point of preserving the books when the stories inside were already lost by not opening them? They'd tried for so long to save the pages, but they were losing the words anyway. It still felt like a betrayal to intentionally sacrifice one, though.

Eric continued tracing his pattern, not caring that it disappeared each time a gust of wind moved the sand. Kyra hadn't even tried to sweep it out, accepting that it was impossible now.

"Maybe it's time to make something new," Eric said softly. "We keep trying to preserve, but..." He touched the wall and a clump of it came off in his hand.

Kyra could picture that happening to the book as she read. Pages turning to dust between her fingers, the spine and cover breaking apart into something unrecognisable. Kyra glanced around her crumbling home. Eric was saying what she'd been thinking but was unable to articulate. Everything was breaking, but letting go still felt impossibly hard.

"Tell me the story you wrote," Eric said suddenly.

"Huh?" Kyra looked up at him.

He hesitated, then reached out, gently touching her arm, tracing his finger along her skin, as if he could still read the lines she had written there.

Why would he want to hear a story she'd made up? She'd spent so long memorising the words of great writers, who had shaped and revised their words into books that were supposed to last forever. Her own stories just swirled inside her mind, she'd had no chance to perfect them.

"I broke my last pen," she told him.

Eric's head bobbed, acknowledging the loss. He had seen the ink on her palms – watched it spread to his own skin when he held her hand.

He gave a half smile. "You're telling me you can memorise whole books, but you can't remember a story you made up without writing it down?"

He had a point. The words had circled in Kyra's head for so long that she knew each of them well, but speaking them aloud was different to just letting them float through her mind.

Eric's fingers traced along her skin again, until he found her hand and squeezed it. "If you won't tell me, then think about telling it at the library," he said.

If she did, she would be telling a story that meant something to the people who came there each day; to the children who were on their own, and the adults who desperately wanted to remember.

Kyra swallowed. "I will think about it," she told Eric, though she wasn't sure she would ever find the courage.

Eric smiled. "After you finish telling them the one about the whale."

THEY MOVED INTO THE library the next day, leaving her broken house behind. They stopped by Eric's place so he could grab a few things; his home was just as broken as hers.

Kyra worried about whether they were allowed to live in the library, but Eric just shrugged. Perhaps someday the council or the other living books would be upset about it, but it had been a long time since anyone other than the two of them had cared about the building or its contents.

Eric stood with Kyra as she stared at the shelf, examining the last of the paper books, finally locating the one about the whale.

"You don't have to," he said. "If you want to just make up the ending, no one will know."

That was true. She was the last person alive who had ever heard the story, her mother being the only one of that generation who had memorised it. Perhaps the version her mother had told her wasn't even the one that was written down. Maybe it had changed over the years, each living book altering it a little, just as the recounts of their histories and the daily news reports changed slightly each time they were told until no one was sure of what was real anymore.

Kyra was starting to realise it didn't matter. The people who came weren't there to hear this *particular* story – they were there to share in a story together, creating new ones even in the listening.

"Tomorrow," she said.

Eric frowned. "Tomorrow?"

"Tomorrow, I will start a new story, one I made up myself. But today we finish the story about the whale."

Eric studied her face for a moment, then he nodded, and carefully lifted the book from the shelf.

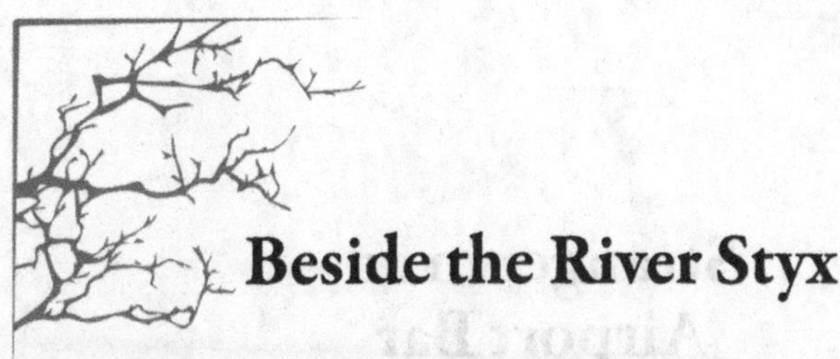

Beside the River Styx

We lay down beside a river. The grass grew around me, tickling my skin as it stretched blades across my body.

I've missed you, you said. You took the coins from my eyes, so I could see.

You held my hand. You asked me what was wrong.

I said I was drowning; you said you were too. We saw ourselves disappear beneath the surface of the river.

The weeds grew up from beneath the water, coiling themselves around my wrists. I told you to let go of my hand; you told me no. My weight dragged you down to the sand of the riverbed.

You'll drown, I said.

You told me you didn't care. Your words turned to bubbles. They floated above our heads, until they popped in the grass.

I'm already dead, I told you.

You shook your head. *We're just asleep*, you said. *We're just dreaming.*

You're just dreaming, I tried to say, but the weeds covered my face.

I won't let you go, you told me.

I know, I said. The grass sliced through my arm.

You dropped my hand as the river swept you downstream.

It's okay, I said, *I want you to let go*. My mouth filled with sand, as the riverbed swallowed me whole.

Stranger in an
Airport Bar

I sat down at the bar and ordered myself a Jack Daniels. My shoulder ached from hauling my "carry-on luggage". Lucky for me they hadn't weighed it. I hated checking bags, so I'd crammed enough for the week into the shoulder bag which was now threatening to dislocate my arm.

My whiskey arrived at the exact same moment a man sat down beside me. A nearly empty bar and he chose the seat next to me. I resisted the urge to shuffle my stool away and focused on my glass instead. He ordered a drink.

In elevators there's that unspoken convention that you don't look at anybody else and just stare straight ahead. It's a rule that should apply to all public places where you're in close proximity to strangers. Well this guy obviously had no idea. He stared at me until I turned and looked at him.

"Hello." He smiled expectantly.

"Hi." I didn't know what else to say. He seemed to want something, but I wasn't sure what it was. "I'm from New Zealand," I said eventually.

"Australia's my home."

"Really?"

"Why would I lie?"

I blinked a couple of times, unsure if I'd misheard him. "Because... I don't know..."

"You have trust issues?"

"Huh?"

"What should I think?"

"Whatever you want." I regretted now not having taken the opportunity to move away when I'd had the chance.

His drink arrived and he took a large swill. "Trust issues it is."

I chuckled despite myself. "I just meant it's odd to fly halfway around the world, then find yourself sitting next to a neighbour."

He stared at me with sleepy, hooded eyes that made me suspect this wasn't his first drink of the night.

I extended my hand. "My name's Ernest."

"Ah, the importance of..."

"Being?"

"Being."

I smiled at the old joke then realised he hadn't given me his name. I went to ask but he continued speaking. "What's your secret?"

"Excuse me?"

He smiled. "Your secret."

I heard a nervous laugh escape my lungs. "How do you know I have one?"

"Everybody has at least one. What are you hiding?"

"Nothing!" The word came out too sharp, too quick.

He held my eye. "Nothing," he repeated softly.

I swallowed and looked down at the bar. He tapped his fingers against his glass as if to music only he could hear.

"So what's *your* secret, then?" I asked.

He chuckled. "Now that would be telling."

"You said everyone had at least one."

"Maybe you'll have to..."

"Guess?"

"Maybe." He took a breath and let it out in something that was not quite a groan, not quite a sigh. "Or perhaps we should tell each other," he said. "On the count of three, unburden ourselves of all that's ailing us."

My mouth felt dry. "I'd rather not..."

"Your choice."

His eyes were closed, and he swayed ever so slightly, trying to keep his equilibrium. He wouldn't remember much of this later; that was obvious. He'd drink himself into a slumber and wake tomorrow wondering how he'd got there.

"My wife thinks I'm on a business trip but I'm really here with another woman." The words came out in a rush before I could stop them.

The man opened his eyes, but he merely nodded. He swallowed the last of his drink and ordered another.

A sickening thought came over me. "You're not a private detective, are you?"

He chuckled again. "No. I'm not."

"Honestly?"

"There's those trust issues again."

I shook my head. "Back to that."

"Always." A smile darted back and forth at the edge of his lips. "You never guessed."

I finished the last of my drink. He was beginning to irritate me. "Help me out..."

"You have no idea, do you?"

"Isn't that obvious?" I felt ready to strangle him.

"Not always."

His second drink came, and he downed it in one. An announcement came over the loudspeakers.

"That's my plane," I said.

"Mine too." He stood, leaning heavily against the bar as he tried to get his balance.

I sighed, hoping he wouldn't be in the seat next to me. "Visiting New Zealand?"

He chuckled. "No good at guessing, are you?"

I shrugged.

He opened his bag and pulled out a jacket and cap. "I'm the pilot," he whispered and pointed to his empty glass. "That's my secret."

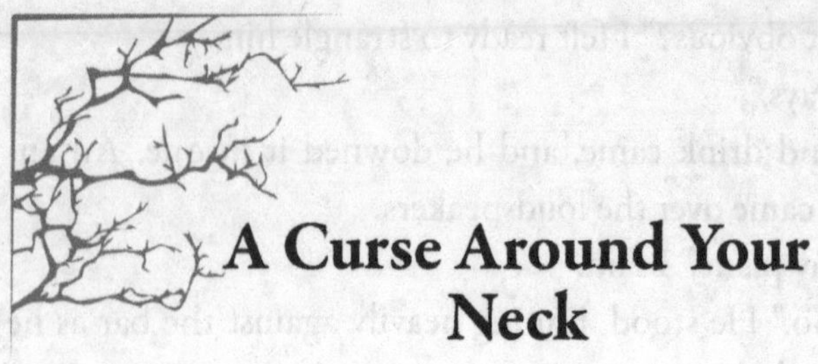

A Curse Around Your Neck

The night before death came calling, our aunt gave our mother a necklace. A thick gold chain, heavy, decadent, and not at all my mother's style.

Thank you, she said anyway as she tried it on. *So kind.*

My aunt's death had nothing to do with the gift. An accident, unfortunate and unrelated, but the necklace sat unworn anyway. Too heavy a reminder of tragedy to be draped around anyone's neck. Heavy, but light enough for fickle fingers to lift. On the tenth anniversary of my aunt's death, the necklace was stolen.

We were selling it – a charity garage sale. Something good to come of something sad. At least that's what we told ourselves, as we tried to unlatch the burden of that grief-laden gift. Our mother had died too by then, and none of us had claimed the gold chain.

Sacrilegious to wear it, we all said, though we knew it wasn't the right word.

It was only later that we recognised the date, and the awful pain it had brought a decade earlier.

We all knew who had stolen it. The woman had been eyeing the necklace, twisting it in her hands like a shining snake as she weighed up the nominal price.

Low to steal from a charity sale, we all said. *Practically wishing a curse upon yourself.*

None of us mentioned the two dead women, who had been the last to loop the chain around their throats. Neither were the type to cast curses, too kind-hearted to wish others ill. But both had been superstitious, recognising omens when they crossed them, and guarding against the fates they called to will.

He Who Laughs Last

T he first was an accident – a joke gone wrong, as they say. Or perhaps a joke gone really right, depending on how you look at it. The second was mostly an accident – maybe an experiment if we're being completely honest. I didn't think I could kill a second time, but I had to try, you know? To see if that first one had been a fluke.

After that, I can't claim innocence. There was intent. There was motive. And the bodies began piling up.

There was a power to it. People didn't normally see me as powerful, and there was something seductive about that. I was used to feeling small – being treated like a child. Funny how not being able to walk makes people see you as little. If you've ever tried to manoeuvre a wheelchair in a bathroom stall, you'll understand how much space I actually take up.

It wasn't just about the power, though. I picked my victims carefully. I'm not saying they deserved to die... All I'm saying is they pissed me off, and sometimes that's the same thing. Of course, with methods like mine, I had to choose my moments carefully, too. Certain medical predispositions helped, but I could make it work without. All it took was favourable – or *un*favourable, depending on your perspective – atmospheric conditions, the right type of food in front of them, and the element of surprise. Surprise was easy. Most people didn't expect me to be funny. They also didn't believe "died laughing" could be literal.

I wheeled into the bar, negotiating the tight doorway. The wind slammed it shut behind me, drawing more attention than I would have liked. I'd had to change locations a lot, to keep from being detected, so I'd got used to navigating all sorts of barely accessible spaces. It had been a good excuse to travel, but the last few months, I'd enjoyed being back in my hometown, even with the Wellington wind adding its own special brand of propulsion to everything I did. I'd be sad when it came time to move on.

If all went to plan, today I'd have my eleventh victim. I already had him picked out – "Gazza" as he insisted everyone call him. He was outside right now, having a cigarette. That gave me a good twenty minutes. When we'd worked together, his smoke breaks had expanded like his ego. Anyone unlucky enough to take theirs at the same time would be caught in a self-serving spiral of bragging anecdotes, as he chain-smoked any cigarettes he could get hold of, whether or not they came from his own pack.

I went to the counter and scanned the ever-expanding list of craft beers, picking out the ones I would try on another night. In Wellington, you had to be a connoisseur of either beer or flat whites to fit in. Tonight, I'd be drinking neither. I needed a clear head, and neither alcohol-fog nor coffee-jitters would help me there.

I ordered a plate of extra-spicy hot wings, and a large bowl of potato wedges. In my experience, peanut butter sandwiches were the best way to induce choking – the target didn't even need to have a peanut allergy. I tried to avoid people with allergies as a general rule; it didn't feel like as much of an achievement to bring them down. But of course, ordering a peanut butter sandwich in a bar would have been a sure-fire way to draw attention to myself, so wedges and spice would have to do.

I hadn't wanted to do too much research. If things ever came to light, a search history of "foods that increase the likelihood of heart attacks" or "choking hazards in adults" wouldn't do me any favours. But I felt safe in assuming solid lumps of potato were among the riskier foods to consume.

I set myself up at a table and waited. Gazza was the easy type of victim. I wouldn't have to persuade him to join me. If I had food in front of me, he would feel entitled to it – entitled to my time and air space too. That's why he'd ended up on my list. He was a bully, and he deserved a good laugh.

I wouldn't have much trouble in that department either. He'd been laughing at me for years.

My food came. The server – Sophie – smiled at me. She placed a bottle of water and a glass on the table beside the food. "You here by yourself tonight, Charlie?" she asked. She'd recently gifted me with her name, and I felt a surge of warmth every time she used mine.

"For now," I said. "I always make friends here."

She smiled again, her face filling with sunshine. "Good on you, Charlie."

I frowned. *Good on you, Charlie.* Patronising? So many people were, sometimes it was hard not to read it into every sentence spoken.

"All else fails, I'll just pick someone up," I said. "They'll have to be my friend if I'm wheeling them away at speed."

Sophie gave a surprised laugh, a delightful hiccupping sound. Her cheeks turned the prettiest shade of pink, and her eyes sparkled. "You're so naughty, Charlie."

I grinned, my own cheeks warming. "Or I could run over their toes. That's a great meet cute."

She let out a whoop. Some of the other customers glanced our way, and Sophie's laugh spluttered into a cough. The pink in her cheeks turned to red, and liquid filled her eyes. My grin fell. I reached for her, handing her the water she had given me just moments before.

She waved it away, still coughing. "Thanks, I'm all good." She cleared her throat, then touched my arm gently, turning back to work.

I watched her carefully as she moved to chat with another customer, her smile warm and easy as she cleared their plates. Kindness filled every movement she made... genuine kindness, not the fake type so often thrown in my direction.

Once upon a time, I would have loved making her laugh. Now something clawed at my stomach, and I wanted to clap a protective hand over her mouth to make her stop. She hadn't been eating, I reminded myself. A laugh could just be a laugh; she wasn't going to choke. Unlike Gazza.

The bar filled, the afterwork throng filing in. This was good. The chaos of a crowd helped take the focus off me. I resisted the urge to stuff one of the wedges in my mouth. Steam spilled from them, and I preferred my tongue unburnt. Though now that I thought about it, a munted tongue and a lisp might add something to my jokes. I'd have to try it out sometime, but tonight was not the night for untested material. Besides, the food had to look appealing when Gazza got inside. I wanted him reaching over to grab a handful, rather than picking at limp leftovers.

The chair beside me scraped back. I looked up, startled, not quite ready for Gazza to join me, but the man beside me was a stranger.

"Hello...?" I said.

He gestured to the chair. "Do you mind?"

"No, you can take it." Not ideal, as I had assumed Gazza would sit there, but there was still a chair to my left. Funny how things like that can throw you. It shouldn't matter whether he sat on my left or my right, but once I'd pictured it one way, it felt wrong to adjust.

The man took off his coat, placing it over the back of the chair, then sat down.

Well. Now this really threw things. I'd thought he wanted to take the chair away, not to sit next to me. I couldn't kill Gazza with a stranger watching on. Or could I? It would be the ultimate test of my abilities. My methods had gone undetected until now, but I'd never tried under such close scrutiny. Could I even get two at once? A double-hitter kill would be quite the achievement.

There was a comfortable rumpledness to the man in front of me, that made me think he might be a father. The untucked end of his shirt drooped down on one side, hinting his waist had expanded since purchasing those pants, and his hair needed a cut. Grey-streaked strands fell across his face in a way that spoke of disorganisation rather than style.

Sophie returned to the table, raising her eyebrows to ask the man's order.

"Just a coke, thanks."

Pleasant enough to thank her – a point in his favour.

"No worries, mate." Sophie smiled at me again as she left, but it didn't have the same warmth as earlier. Her hand snuck to her temple, rubbing it gently, before she turned to another customer.

An image of her crying flashed through my mind. Maybe I should have waited until a night she wasn't working. She'd be the type to blame herself, you know? Even if she thought it was an accident. Another flash followed – her head on my shoulder, the tears falling on my neck. My arms wrapping around to comfort her...

I dropped my gaze to my food as she caught me staring.

"I've seen you before."

I turned back to the man. Often, that sort of statement had a question mark at the end – not really a query in and of itself, but an invitation to conversation.

"I come here a lot," I said. I kept my voice flat, invitation declined.

"Good on you." The man stared at me, a slight smile teasing the corners of his mouth, as if we were sharing a joke.

I didn't return it. I'd given Sophie the benefit of the doubt, but the words were definitely patronizing from *his* lips – a congratulations for being capable of frequenting a bar. I got comments of a similar nature a lot. Leaving the house is apparently noteworthy when using a wheelchair. Sophie returned with his coke, and he thanked her.

My wedges had cooled, and I picked one up, admiring the solid cut and greasy coating. Under different circumstances, I would have turned up my nose, but these were perfect for my purposes.

The man watched me eat it, with far more interest than was warranted. His lip quirked into another smile as I swallowed.

Clearly, leaving the house wasn't the only thing he was surprised I could do independently. I waited for him to congratulate me on ingesting food without choking.

I pushed the plate towards him. "Would you like some?"

He hesitated. Something flicked across his face, and for a moment, I could have sworn he was afraid. Then it was gone, replaced by the familiar smile.

"Thanks, friend," he said. He took a napkin from the metal pail in the centre of the table, laying it in front of him, then he grabbed a wedge and broke it in two before eating. Sensible. Smaller pieces certainly reduced the choking hazard. I allowed myself to feel a touch of disappointment.

He held out his hand. "You can call me Mike."

"Charlie."

His smile widened at that, and I couldn't help thinking I should have given a fake name. Not that anyone would find anything suspicious about Gazza's death, but anonymity couldn't hurt.

"You here alone tonight?" he asked.

"Yeah, alone," I said. Without thinking, my gaze travelled towards Sophie. I forced it back, but his attention had followed mine.

"But I saw someone I used to work with outside," I said quickly. "He might join me."

What was I doing? Why had I told him I used to work with Gazza? Not smart, Charlie. Not smart at all.

"I've never been here before." Mike glanced at something over my shoulder. I didn't turn to look, but I knew it would be Sophie. His smile stretched into a leer. "I might just have to become a regular."

A roiling wave of heat rose inside me, and my ears pulsed. *Don't look at her like that!* I wanted to yell, but I had no claim to the moral high ground. Just moments ago, I'd been fantasising about comforting her over Gazza's literal dead body.

I shook my head to clear it. Choosing Sophie's bar had been a risk, but maybe not for the reason I'd thought. I couldn't think straight when she was around.

Where was Gazza? His exorbitantly long cigarette breaks weren't unfamiliar, especially if he'd found someone to indulge his storytelling, but this one had dragged out even for him.

I glanced back at Mike. He stared at me, his gaze intent... almost expectant. I picked up one of the spicy wings, to give myself something to do. Mike leaned forward, watching.

I fumbled under the scrutiny, the slimy barbeque sauce slipping between my fingers. The corners of Mike's lips curled again, the smile unnerving. The wing finally reached my mouth, but my appetite dissolved. I nibbled on the chicken before setting it down.

"Would you like one?" I asked Mike.

His smile turned into a baring-of-teeth grin. "Yeah, nah, I'll pass thank you. Never been a fan of spice." He reached for another wedge, breaking it into pieces once again.

I couldn't say I was a fan of the spice either. I didn't need to see my face to know the intricate pattern of blood vessels under my skin had flushed crimson. Sometimes I fell victim to my own methods.

"You're here a lot, Charlie."

I frowned. Mike said my name like we knew each other. I studied his face, but there was nothing familiar there. He stared back just as intently, then he turned to look at Sophie. "Won a heart there, have you?"

I let out a breath, and a new wave of heat painted my skin. "I... I'm a regular."

Mike chuckled. "A regular. That's a good term for it."

I frowned. Why was that funny? His tone was amiable, but something cold glinted in his eyes. Whatever the joke, I wished he would let me in on it.

I edged my chair back. People filled the room, but at least three tables stood empty around the other end of the bar. Why had he chosen to sit with me? He leaned forward, closing the gap I'd created between us. His stare locked me in, making it impossible to look away.

"You said you'd seen me," I said.

"I have."

"But you've never been here before." My throat felt raw, and not just from the spice.

Mike's smile turned sly. He took a slug of his coke as if he was downing a shot of whiskey. "I have. I've been watching you for a while."

I blinked, wondering if I'd misheard him. "Excuse me?"

His rumpledness didn't look so comfortable anymore. Hard edges seemed to form on his features as I watched. I looked for Sophie, but another customer held her attention.

Mike followed my gaze once again. "Sweet girl. Let's not involve her in this."

"What *is* this?" Sweat dampened my temples and my shirt. *You can call me Mike.* Odd wording – a fake name, for sure.

He grabbed another wedge, placing it on the napkin in front of him, then took a knife from the pail. He cut the potato in half, examining the pieces, but he didn't eat them. I had the distinct impression it had simply been an excuse to pick up a weapon.

"You know how many people I've seen die, Charlie?"

"What?" I could barely force the word out.

Sophie crossed the bar. Her movements seemed to crawl, but somehow, she was still getting further away from me. I wanted to yell for her. I wanted her to come and save me.

"Five. Most of them on the job."

Oh god, he was a cop. But how? I'd been so careful. Or had I? I'd been getting complacent lately, sure I was undetectable. How could they link me to the deaths? I'd never touched any of them; I'd just made them laugh. That wasn't a crime.

"So imagine our surprise when we keep hearing about this man in a wheelchair at the scenes of seven deaths around the country in the last year."

I'd been stupid, so stupid. They hadn't even caught me for all of them, but they would. They would. They would find those other victims, and I'd be done. It was over, it was all over.

"Funny thing is, they were non-suspicious deaths. See, that's even rarer. Most of the people who see a lot of death, it's suspicious as hell."

I clasped the wheels of my chair. "Mike" reached out, snapping on the brake. He carried on as if he hadn't moved.

"No known poisons in their systems, no visible wounds, eyewitnesses who all say no one touched them... yet there you were, sitting next to each one of them as they died."

I reached for the brake, but he caught my hand. I watched Sophie, like a lifeline, but I'd floated too far from her. Would she help me? Would she still smile if she knew what I'd done?

"The thing we still can't work out is how you did it."

He almost laughed when he said "you". Even now, knowing what I'd done, he still saw me as weak. He looked at me with disgust, but a light sparked in his eyes – eagerness, or maybe a hint of admiration. He wanted to know, not because he was a cop, but because he was jealous.

"I don't know what you're talking about." I surprised myself with the steady tone of my voice. I sat up straighter, suddenly confident in my safety. Making someone laugh wasn't a crime. He had circumstantial evidence at best.

The slow smile crept over Mike's face again, and my new-found confidence wavered. "Yes, you do, Charlie. We know you do."

Out of the corner of my eye, I saw the door to the courtyard open. My heart pounded, matching Gazza's steps as he strode over to me, just as I had hoped he would. Mike's smile turned back into a baring of teeth.

Gazza grinned too when he saw me, a cat spying a small creature he could play with. Light glinted off his forehead, hitting the sheen of sweat he'd built up from the prolonged period of breathing smoke instead of air.

Run, I wanted to yell. *Run, Gazza, get away while you can.* But I had been going to kill him tonight. He should be running from me, not just from Mike.

He flopped himself down in the chair to my left. "Got some company tonight, have you Charlie?"

"This is Mike," I choked out.

Gazza's eye travelled over Mike, assessing and finding to his liking. Someone like Gazza would always prefer to talk to people like Mike – normal people. On another day, they would have been friends, ganging up to make fun of me.

"Kia ora, mate. Call me Gazza." He held out his right hand, slapping Mike on the shoulder with the other. "What are you doing with little Charlie here?"

Mike shrugged. "Charlie's got some interesting talents I'm curious to know more about."

If I'd been able to see myself, I'm sure I would have been turning green.

"Talents? Charlie?" Gazza let out a guffawing laugh. "What, are you hiring for a freak show?"

Mike frowned, his distaste for the joke evident. "Nothing like that. I work in a... specialised line of work."

"He's a cop," I blurted out.

"A cop?" Gazza's laughter turned to wheezing.

If I'd still been trying to kill him, this would have been the perfect moment. Another one-liner, before he could catch his breath, and he'd be gasping his way to the floor. Nausea and the rasping pain of spice burns battled it out in my throat, neither leaving room for jokes.

Gazza shook his head. "You're barking up the wrong tree, mate. Charlie's a right crack up – wouldn't think it to look at him – but he ain't going to help you with police work."

Mike's lips turned thin, the smile forced, as he glanced between the two of us. "You'd be surprised what Charlie can do." There it was again – that hint of admiration in his voice.

"I'm telling you, mate. Little Charlie's useless. Look at the kid!"

Gazza and I were the same age, not that you could tell by looking at us. Indulgence had aged him well beyond his years, but he'd fooled himself into thinking the difference in our appearance came from me looking young.

Mike regarded Gazza coolly. He took a pen from his pocket, doodling on the napkin he'd used earlier. "I just came to get a feel for Charlie's skill. I'm sure you're right – nothing to brag about."

Mike tossed the napkin down, as if over the whole thing, but I knew that tone of voice. It was the one we'd all used in the office to placate Gazza into silence.

Gazza picked up one of my hot wings. Mike leaned forward, sudden energy filling his face. His eyes flicked to the greasy chicken, following Gazza's hand as he lifted it to his lips.

Gazza tore the meat from the bone with his teeth. "Now, me..." he said, his mouth full. "I'd make a great cop."

Mike's gaze slid back to me, a question in his eyes. He thought I'd used poison. That's why he'd refused the wings. We both watched Gazza take another bite, Mike waiting for a death, me for an opportunity to escape. Gazza tossed the stripped bone onto the plate.

Mike sat back in his chair, his face crinkling into a frown. I wondered at the fact he hadn't intervened. Did he actually *want* me to kill Gazza? I shook my head. Not today, Mikey. I wasn't that stupid. He'd as good as admitted they had no case against me. If I killed Gazza now, circumstantial would turn to actual evidence. If I played this right, I'd be home free.

"You're quiet, Charlie-boy," Gazza said. "No jokes tonight?"

Mike's fingers drummed an irritated rhythm on the tabletop. He picked up the napkin, tapping it against the table in an expansion of his personal percussion. The sheen of sweat on Gazza's face had turned to a flood with the spice. He rubbed his chest, as if the hot wing had given him instant heartburn.

"I..." My eye fell on the napkin in Mike's hand. He'd folded it into a point, which now aimed at Gazza, and he'd scrawled our names on the end of it. *Charlie Mike.* That meant something, didn't it? Some military term?

They both stared at me, friendly expectation filling Gazza's face, but something darker and more urgent crossing Mike's.

"No jokes tonight," I repeated.

Charlie Mike... C. M.

Mike looked from me to Gazza, then pointedly down at the food.

C. M.... Continue... mission?

Suddenly, I saw it all through Mike's eyes – unexplained deaths, no hint of harm or cause. He wasn't trying to catch me; he thought I was an expert in chemicals or weapons... something he could learn from.

I just came to get a feel for Charlie's skill. Maybe he really did want me to kill Gazza. I should do it. Make them all laugh, and watch Gazza drop dead of the heart attack he'd been threatening for months.

Gazza reached for a wedge, again with both Mike's and my eyes trailing his movements. He popped the whole thing between his teeth. I opened my mouth, but nothing came out. No jokes, no quippy comments, not even a non-sequitur odd enough to prompt a surprised laugh.

I picked up a wedge of my own. The idea of eating churned my stomach, but I put it in my mouth anyway, chewing over all I knew about "Mike" as the food rolled across my tongue.

What would he make of my methods? He came here looking for an assassin; what would he do when he found a comedian instead? *I'm sorry, sir. I don't know how to use a gun, but would you like to hear a knock-knock joke?*

I started to laugh, a big bubble of it building from my chest. Gazza joined me, so ready for my humour he didn't even need to hear the joke. I gasped. The irony. He didn't know how funny his death would have been. I leaned forward, tears streaming from my eyes.

"So good you can't even get the punchline out, eh?"

I nodded, cackling at just how good it would have been. I opened my mouth to tell them, and the half-eaten wedge slipped back into my throat.

I spluttered, a sound I had heard from all of my victims, as my jokes lodged food in their windpipes.

Gazza chuckled. "You right, little man?"

I clasped my throat, the sign for choking, which I had pretended not to see so many times. Mike slowly shook his head, something close to admiration growing on his face. He thought I'd done this on purpose.

Underneath the sweat, Gazza's skin paled, turning a waxy grey. "Sophie," he yelled. "Call 111!"

I gurgled, saliva pooling in my mouth. Sophie met my eye across the bar, her face paling too. She grabbed the phone and ran towards me, her thumb punching the three numbers without looking. And then someone was pulling me from my chair, slapping me on the back, but it was too late. The stodge of potato had expanded to fill my spice-swollen throat.

Mike stood, putting his jacket back on. He stretched, then turned towards the door, his pace casual. I'd made similar exits myself, slipping away as the crowd tried to save my victim.

Sophie fumbled with the phone, and a customer took it from her. Black spots peppered my vision, blocking out her face.

"Ambulance, hurry!" the woman said.

Wait, I wanted to call after Mike. *Wait, it wasn't me! I didn't do anything. I just made them laugh.*

He looked back at me, and suddenly the dishevelled father had returned, smiling kindly at me. He almost seemed sad.

A tear rolled down my cheek. Moisture filled Sophie's eyes too. It was so close to how I had planned it. Her tears, falling on Gazza's neck as she leaned her head on his shoulder. His arms, wrapping around to comfort her.

I blinked, darkness crowding in. *Charlie died doing what he loved – laughing,* my eulogy would say, and everyone at the funeral would laugh too, with tears in their eyes. Maybe one of them would even keel over, the two of us the final victims for my list.

The Woman Next Door

The woman next door was not human. The first clue was the seal in her backyard. It could have been mistaken for a dog, but its bark was accompanied by the slap and splash of flippers on water.

"That dog's her familiar," Clara said.

"It's a seal," said Talia, but Clara shook her head.

"It's a plain old dog, but she's done gone magicked it. It's in disguise, just like her."

The woman's disguise came with legs, but she still smelt of salt. Her hands were speckled brown like sun-baked sand, and they bent and twisted like driftwood. Talia caught glimpses of her hair over the fence – long strands of icy white, peppered with streaks of charcoal and sometimes blue. It rippled out in waves when the wind caught it, almost like she was trying to make her own ocean in place of the one she'd lost.

Sometimes she'd catch Talia staring, and she'd give her a look. One that said she knew. Clara called her a witch, and Talia longed to have magic like hers. She longed to see the sea up close, not just from a carpark near, but never on, the beach.

"Don't look her in the eye," Clara whispered. "She'll get you if you look her in the eye."

Talia didn't believe her sister, but she stared at the ground the next time the woman looked her way all the same. Talia's hands clutched at the handles of her crutches, ready to make the fastest slow-getaway she could muster.

The woman sang beautifully, a sad song with words Talia didn't understand. Talia leaned against the fence listening, delicious waves of melancholy washing over her.

Clara covered her ears. "Don't listen," she hissed. "She'll draw you in like a siren and cook you in her oven." There was a gleam in Clara's eye – the same one she got when she made up stories about monsters under the bed.

"Mermaids don't eat people." Talia clapped her hands over her mouth. She had not meant to give away the woman's secret.

Clara's smile grew wider. "Shows how much you know. They do, and she's a witch not a mermaid, anyhow."

Talia let Clara have the victory. Perhaps mermaids did eat people, but only sailors who tried to catch them.

The woman wore brightly coloured long dresses that swirled around her ankles, though her steps were small, and she walked with a limp. Talia liked listening to her move. The shush of her right foot sweeping along the concrete created a soothing rhythm, like water rushing in and out, in and out.

"Witches melt when they get wet," Clara said.

The gleam in her eye was back, lighting up at the thought of their neighbour dissolving into a puddle of swirling colour. She grabbed the hose and sent a spray of rainbow-lit droplets over the top of the fence. Talia peered through the gaps between the boards, watching for any sign of a tail.

The woman shrieked, letting out a stream of muffled words that could only be curses.

Clara dropped the hose, only brave enough to face a liquid witch, not one who dared to stay solid. "Run!" Clara yelled.

Talia grabbed her crutches, but Clara didn't wait. She disappeared into the house, leaving Talia to face the woman alone.

Her hair appeared first, long floating clouds of white and blue strands rising over the top of the fence. Then her face, brown-speckled skin bunched up into lines, wrinkles deepened by a frown.

She peered at Talia with one eye, the other clamped tightly shut against the brightness of the setting sun. "You been watering over my fence, huh?"

Talia shook her head. Her throat burned as the woman looked her up and down.

"That sister of yours, then. Left you here, huh? That one's a mischievous bratling."

Talia nodded. The woman cracked a little smile, and she watched Talia with her one-eyed gaze. Talia snuck looks at her. Clara was wrong. The woman wouldn't "get her", but her magic was too strong to look at all the same.

The woman stepped down from her perch on the fence, opening the gate. It swung wide, revealing the green of grass and the deep, deep blue of a wide pool on the other side. Talia inched forward, gaping at the colours.

"Come on in with you, then." The woman nodded her head towards her garden.

Talia hesitated. Witch or mermaid, the woman was still the strangest of strangers.

"Suit yourself." The woman turned away, reaching to close the gate.

Talia jerked forward, pulling her crutches into a clumsy lurch. The woman made a harrumphing sound in her throat, but she held off on closing the gate, letting Talia pass through.

"Sit yourself by the pool," she said. "Cool your feet."

Talia eased herself down to sit on the tiles, pulling off her shoes, and resting her crutches beside her. A sleepy ball of fur shifted as she did. The pup jumped into the water, barking and splashing as if inviting Talia to play.

"Ah, he's a silly old badger," the woman said. She creaked her way down to the ground across from Talia, letting her feet dangle in the water too. Her right ankle bent sideways, knobbly bones visible through her skin. Both of the woman's eyes were open, now, and bright, black pupils studied Talia from below a heavy frown. "What's your sister doing watering me, then?" she asked.

Talia shrank, wishing she was the one who would melt. "She thinks you're a witch."

"A witch, huh?" The woman chuckled to herself. "Do you think I'm one too?"

Talia shook her head. "I think you're a mermaid."

"A mermaid..." Her lips quirked into a smile.

The pup swam towards Talia, his little tail splashing behind him. Talia reached out a hand, letting her fingers trace ripples across the surface as he passed her.

The woman stood, leaning heavily on the rail beside the pool. She waded her way into the water, her long dress flowing out around her. Talia watched the woman's legs, but the fabric twisted and swirled around them, hiding her skin from view.

"Come," the woman said. "You're like me. You'll move better in the water than on land." She reached out her hands to Talia, drawing her into the depths.

Talia glanced at her crutches, then back at the woman. She let her neighbour lower her into the pool. Talia's dress rippled out around her, just like the woman's, turning Talia's bent limbs into a tail. "You *are* a mermaid," she whispered.

The woman's face crinkled. "What's a mermaid but a witch in the water, and what's a witch but an old lady people label crazy?"

Talia didn't dare look down, but she was sure she could feel silky scales growing on her skin, and the tingle of magic bubbling around them.

CLARA SLUNK AROUND the house that night, hiding behind furniture and doorways as if her shame wasn't visible through them.

"She doesn't melt," Talia said. "I told you she's a mermaid, not a witch."

Clara sneered. "She ain't nothing magical, just a crazy old bat."

Talia smiled. Her sister could believe what she wanted, but Talia knew the truth. The woman was a mermaid. Talia had seen the seal pup that proved it.

The Night Village

The figure leaning over me was pale, unnaturally so. Dark eyes stared down at me, the pupils enlarged to the point of swallowing the colour.

"Cora..." she whispered.

"No!" I flung out a hand. My fingers tangled in her hair and brittle strands crawled across my skin. She leaned closer, and the ends brushed my face, creeping down over my throat as if they would strangle me.

I sucked in a breath to scream, but long bony fingers pressed to my lips. "It's okay. Cora, it's me. Wake up."

My hand closed around the cold silicone of my phone, and it lit up. The figure reeled backwards, shielding her eyes.

"God, Cora, I was trying to help! Turn that off."

I blinked. "Sarah?"

"Light. Off," she hissed.

I stabbed a fingertip at the phone's screen. It read my intent, switching to nocturnal mode. The cool white light faded to a dim red, just enough to see by.

Sarah slowly lowered her hands. Her eyelids fluttered, the solid black pupils contracting briefly then widening out into the inky wells that had stared down at me earlier.

"I'm sorry," she said. "I heard you having a nightmare. I thought you might be..."

"No, *I'm* sorry. I didn't mean to—" I cut myself off. I'd been about to say I didn't mean to wake her, because that's what I always said. When I screamed in my sleep. When I woke everyone by crashing mindlessly through the house or running into a wall to escape my tangled dreams. But Sarah hadn't been asleep. That was the point.

"Hey, it's okay." She reached out, squeezing my hand.

Mine were sweating, my clammy palms a product of the terrifying waking dreams I was already forgetting. Or perhaps signs of something else.

Sarah checked the monitor attached to my side. It was beeping, but I hadn't woken with the alarm. Sarah adjusted something on the keypad, and I felt my heartrate slow.

The new-generation medications worked quickly, but only if you took them on time. Normally, my haphazard sleep meant I was too late, the monitor sending an emergency alert before I registered something was wrong.

Sarah gently smoothed my twisted sheets. "Let's go for a walk. You'll feel better with some air."

My breath came out in something that was half sigh, half laugh. A walk in the middle of the night. What a novelty.

"Is it safe?"

Sarah laughed. "You daylighters are such nervous nellies. Get dressed. It will be fine, you'll see."

I PULLED ON SOME WARMER clothes then peeled the black-out shield away from the window. I was surprised to see the road outside was only dimly lit. The streetlights cast a hazy glow which barely penetrated the night air. Naively, I'd thought the Night Village would be lit up to mimic daylight, letting the inhabitants live as normal, just to a different time frame. Of course, that would defeat the purpose of separating the population. There would be no easing of the strain on the infrastructure if resources were in use 24/7.

"You ready?" Sarah called from the hallway.

I turned away from the window, following Sarah outside.

She led me down the street. I shadowed her closely, unable to shake the ingrained fear that bad things happened at night. Wasn't it the mantra our parents had always taught us? *Don't go out after dark; it's not safe.*

Sarah seemed to sense my hesitation and slipped her arm through mine. I winced as she brushed against the bruises on my ribs. She must have seen the matching set on my face, even in the low light. I wasn't kidding myself that she had suggested this sleepover simply because she missed me. She knew my sleepwalking had reached dangerous levels again.

"Are you hungry? There's a great café down here."

I grinned. "Midnight snack?"

Sarah blinked, the term taking a moment to register. "Just lunch," she said quietly.

I swallowed. I kept forgetting that this was not the unique experience for her that it was for me. Would this really be her life forever? Awake during the night, never seeing the sun again?

"Sure," I said.

THE CAFÉ WAS CALLED The Social Insomniac. I cracked a smile and wondered if Sarah had brought me here simply for the name. The place seemed cosy, like it was filled with regulars. People who had once been strangers but were now companions meeting nightly over their midnight coffees.

We took our lunch to go, wandering through the streets until we came to a park.

"How are you feeling now?" Sarah asked. She cast a glance at my monitor, but no more alerts sounded.

"Better," I said. This was a novelty too – recovering easily after a medical episode. If only I could learn to wake with the alerts and not just my terrifying dreams.

I shivered, and Sarah wrapped an arm around me. "You get used to the cold," she told me. "You get used to all of it."

I nodded, because what else could I do? Even if she didn't get used to it, she had been assigned to live here. She had no choice but to comply.

I watched the people around us. I'd expected everyone to carry the same physical changes as Sarah – the skin pallor from lack of sun exposure, the widened pupils. But it seemed the effects wore off after a while. With vitamin D supplements, everyone would be fine. Vitamin D and whatever chemicals everyone here had to take to switch their circadian rhythms to favour a nocturnal cycle.

"Are you happy here, Soph?"

Suddenly, I felt a desperate need to know she was okay. Like many other daylighters, I carried a guilt at being allowed to stay in sunlight when so many had been conscripted to darkness.

Sarah didn't answer for a moment. She stared out towards the edge of the Night Village. My home was just over the border, carefully chosen so I would be close enough to visit. So many friendships had slowly dissolved, the time difference too great, even when the physical distance was measured in metres.

"Some people are moving here voluntarily," Sarah said finally.

"Really?" I wasn't sure that answered my question about whether or not she was happy, but presumably it couldn't be that bad if people were choosing it.

"Not everyone takes the nocturnal meds."

I turned to look at her. "I thought you had to."

Sarah gave a wry smile. "You daylighters. Always such sticklers for the rules."

Wouldn't that make life harder? The whole point was that everyone woke and slept at the same time, so that they could build community. Or at least that's what they told us. The real reason was to ease the strain overpopulation had put on the city's power grid and other infrastructure, but that didn't sound as pretty.

Without the meds, people would be...

Without the meds, people would be like me in the daylight world, awake at the wrong time. Or rather, awake in the wrong place.

"There are others like you, Cora," Sarah said.

"Like me?" Suddenly, it made sense why Sarah had invited me to stay.

"Insomniacs. People with sleep disorders. Other health problems."

I thought of the café – The Social Insomniac. How many times had I wished for a place to go when my night terrors woke me, or when I was having a bad day with my health and was afraid going to sleep would mean not waking up again?

How many times had I ached to call someone for help, only to be put off by the thought of waking them? No matter how often people assured me they wouldn't mind, I couldn't escape the feeling I was a burden. And of course, I woke them anyway, my screams dragging them from slumber faster than any request ever could.

But here...

"I am happy," Sarah told me. "I promise. You could be too."

She slipped her hand into mine. Was it really that simple? Could I finally find my place in a world built for insomniacs?

I stared back towards the border of the Night Village. In the distance, the sun was rising. Around us a few people paused, watching colours light the sky as the daylight world began to wake.

"I always did like the night," I said.

A Note From The Author

Thank you for reading *Beside the River Styx*. These stories came about over a number of years, and it's been so much fun revisiting them and putting together this collection.

Did you enjoy this book? You can make a big difference. Reviews are the most powerful tool when it comes to getting attention for my books.

As an indie author, it can be hard to get my books into the hands of readers, but honest reviews help me do just that.

If you've enjoyed this book, I would be very grateful if you could spend just a few minutes leaving a review (it can be as short as you like.)

Thank you very much!

Want more short stories?

A WOMAN FINDS A DEATH Curse symbol scratched into the soap scum around her sink. A young boy watches his family fall apart after the death of his father. A butterfly chrysalis hatches under the watchful eye of a hungry cat, and a teenage grim reaper's job is made harder by the boy who can see her.

Sad, poignant, and darkly funny tales about death. If you like unique points of view, heart-breaking moments, and a touch of black humour, then you'll love Helen Vivienne Fletcher's first short story collection, *Symbolic Death*.

Get it for free when you sign up for Helen's newsletter at www.helenvfletcher.com

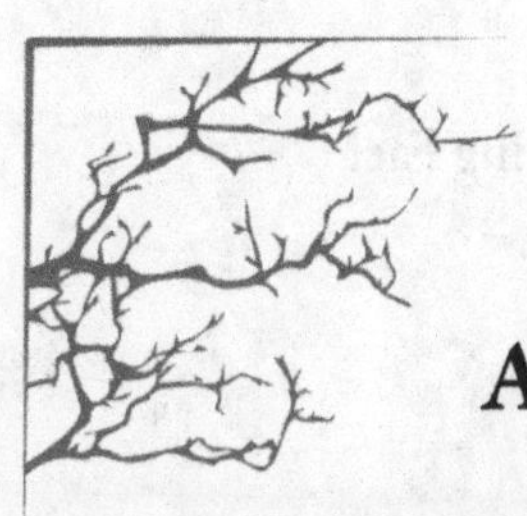

Also by Helen

Reactive Magic Series

Reactive

Magnetic

Volatile

Explosive

Reactive Magic: The Complete Series

.

Familiar Magic Series

Familiars and Foes

Accidents and Apparitions (published in Jingle Spells)

Curses and Cousins

.

Young Adult Books

Broken Silence

Underwater

We All Fall

.

Children's Books

The Trespassers Club

There's No Such Thing As Humans

Aunt Kelly's Dog

Jenny No-Knickers
Do Fruit Worry About Getting Fat?

.

Short Stories
Symbolic Death
Beside the River Styx
Find out more at www.helenvfletcher.com

About the Author

Helen Vivienne Fletcher is a children's and young adult author, spoken word poet and award-winning playwright. She has won and been shortlisted for numerous writing competitions including winning the Outstanding New Playwright Award at the Wellington Theatre Awards, making the shortlist for the Storylines Joy Cowley Award, and the finalist list for the Ngaio Marsh Best First Book Award.

Helen has worked in many jobs, doing everything from theatre stage management to phone counselling. She discovered her passion for writing for young people while working as a youth support worker, and now helps children find their own passion for storytelling through her work as a creative writing tutor.

She lives in Wellington with her disability assistance dog, Bindi – a five-year-old, playful Labrador who loves soft toys, cuddles, and can fit three tennis balls in her mouth at once.

Overall, Helen just loves telling stories and is always excited when people want to read or hear them.

Read more at https://www.helenvfletcher.com/.